WELCOME TO
PASSPORT TO READING
A beginning reader's ticket to a brand-new world!

Every book in this program is designed to build read-along and read-alone skills, level by level, through engaging and enriching stories. As the reader turns each page, he or she will become more confident with new vocabulary, sight words, and comprehension.

These PASSPORT TO READING levels will help you choose the perfect book for every reader.

READING TOGETHER
Read short words in simple sentence structures together to begin a reader's journey.

READING OUT LOUD
Encourage developing readers to sound out words in more complex stories with simple vocabulary.

READING INDEPENDENTLY
Newly independent readers gain confidence reading more complex sentences with higher word counts.

READY TO READ MORE
Readers prepare for chapter books with fewer illustrations and longer paragraphs.

This book features sight words from the educator-supported Dolch Sight Words List. This encourages the reader to recognize commonly used vocabulary words, increasing reading speed and fluency.

For more information, please visit passporttoreadingbooks.com.

Enjoy the journey!

Little, Brown and Company

Hachette Book Group
1290 Avenue of the Americas, New York, NY 10104
Visit us at lb-kids.com
mylittlepony.com

Little, Brown and Company is a division of Hachette Book Group, Inc.
The Little, Brown name and logo are trademarks of Hachette Book Group, Inc.

The publisher is not responsible for websites (or their content) that are not owned by the publisher.

First Edition: September 2015

ISBN 978-0-316-41081-6

10 9 8 7 6 5 4 3 2 1

CW

Printed in the United States of America

Passport to Reading titles are leveled by independent reviewers applying the standards developed by Irene Fountas and Gay Su Pinnell in *Matching Books to Readers: Using Leveled Books in Guided Reading*, Heinemann, 1999.

Licensed By:

WE LIKE SPIKE!

by **Jennifer Fox**

LITTLE, BROWN AND COMPANY
New York Boston

Attention, My Little Pony fans!
Look for these words when you read this book.
Can you spot them all?

dragon

breath

heroes

gem

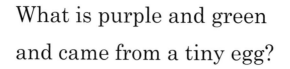

What is purple and green
and came from a tiny egg?

It is our friend Spike!

He is a dragon.

Spike is not big or scary
like other dragons.

He is a cute little guy.

He is a great friend
and a super assistant.

Spike uses his magic fire breath
to send scrolls.

He is always ready to help.

Spike works really hard.

He also knows how to have fun!

Spike likes to read comic books.

His favorite heroes

are the Power Ponies.

He likes to laugh and
can be very silly!

Our little Spike is a total sweetheart.

He also has a sweet tooth!

Spike bakes yummy gem cakes.

Most of the gems do not
end up in the cake!
They end up in his belly!

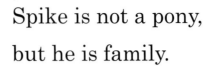

Spike is not a pony,
but he is family.

We like Spike!